The Dog
Who Couldn't Make Up
His Mind

by

I-J Letters

**Grosvenor House
Publishing Limited**

This book is published by
Grosvenor House Publishing Ltd
Link House
140 The Broadway, Tolworth, Surrey, KT6 7HT.
www.grosvenorhousepublishing.co.uk

This book is a work of fiction. Any resemblance to
people or events, past or present, is purely coincidental.

A CIP record for this book
is available from the British Library

ISBN 978-1-83975-183-7

Once upon a time, there was a Dog. He was a very nice Dog, a very friendly Dog and extremely good natured. 'For the life of me,' he said, scratching his floppy ears and twitching his snout.
'I cannot make up my mind, no matter how hard I try. The sun is beaming, the little birds are twittering in the trees, I really ought to wag my tail and go somewhere. Yes and do something special.'

Life normally treated Dog very well indeed but on this particular summer's day he could not make up his mind. He had tossed and turned and thought and thought but nothing came to him.

You see, for some reason, it was a big problem today. As he looked up to the sky he remarked, 'My, my, on a day like today, I simply must do something very special.' Dog stretched and yawned beneath the beautiful bright sunshine. 'Hmmm,' he said, 'I think I shall lie down for a while and think about what I may do'.
As Dog lay basking in the sunshine, he considered his plans.

'I could go down to the seaside,' he thought aloud. 'Or perhaps go to the countryside'. The seaside and the countryside were delightful places.

Both of these seemed to be very good ideas to Dog.

'Perhaps I could go to both of them! If I went to the seaside, I could swim in the sea, oh, and perhaps catch some lovely fresh fish for my supper and collect

some pretty pebbles and shells for my friends
and even build a kennel in the sand and then go
on a boat trip. But oh dear, I wouldn't have any time
left in the day to visit the countryside.'

Dog sat in his chair and thought and thought. 'I shall
go to the seaside, that's decided. But oh dear me, I do
love a day in the country. If I went there, I could go for
a lovely long walk through woods and deep into the forest
and enjoy the scents of wild flowers and berries and
collect some for my friends as I went. Then I may pick
a nice spot by the babbling brook and lay out a picnic
on my favourite rug and on

my return I could visit some old chums and
take flowers to my Great Aunt, as she lives
close by. 'Oh, that sounds perfect.' He sat back
down and shrugged. 'I simply don't know what
would be best. What a puzzle this is and quite tiring.
I think I'll have a snooze.'

Perhaps my dreams will help me to decide and after
all,' he yawned. 'It's such a warm day, mustn't let it
go to waste.' And, with that said, he drifted off to
sleep sprawled out on his lawn.

'Ouch' said the dog with a startled woof.
'What was that?' 'just me' said the bumble bee,

'I thought you would be going somewhere nice today
as it's very hot and sunny. You have been sleeping for ages.
I thought you might like to know.'

'Oh, thank you, I suppose,' grouched Dog as sometimes
he was a little grumpy when he woke up.

'So Bumblebee … what time is it anyway?'

'It's after eleven o'clock, almost midday. You had better get a move on …if you're going. I am very busy you know, making the most of my time. I have lots of flowers to visit, honey to make for you. You do know how busy life is for me. Well …?'

'Yes, yes Buzzy face but not yet' said Dog 'I have to have my elevenses' first.'

'Hurry then I don't know what your problem is' buzzed Bee. 'I can't decide where to go,' moaned Dog 'and anyway, munching on biscuits always helps me to think.'

'Fair enough dear Dog, everyone is different,' and so Bumblebee flew away to visit a bright, inviting buttercup.

And with that . . .

. . . Dog drifted back
to sleep.

8

'Ah!' shrieked Dog, 'Whatever was that?'

'Only me', hissed the familiar voice of Cat.

'Oh, what do you want? It's much too warm for me to go chasing after you and anyway, I was fast asleep. You should know better than to wake me from my slumber,' groaned Dog.

'Oh, I'm very sorry but I didn't expect to find you here,' said Cat.

'Whatever do you mean? I live here!' said Dog. 'Yes . but on a beautiful day like today. I would have thought you would have gone away somewhere', said Cat.

'I am going away … somewhere. I just haven't decided where I am going,' said Dog. 'You see I have so many ideas and I cannot decide.'

'Ah, I see, well you had better hurry up dear Dog.'

'Why?' said Dog.

'It's almost dinner time!' said Cat grinning.

'Oh no, no, no,' gasped Dog. 'Oh yes, yes, yes,' said Cat with sympathy. 'Hurry, hurry Dog, I shall see you tomorrow. I have an urgent meeting with Mouse,' and leaving Dog chasing his tail, she slinked away through the hedgerow. 'Ayah,' screeched Cat, 'Out of my way you pesky hedgehog. You should be awake it's summertime, you know! 'Yes, I do know but it's not dark-time yet,' giggled Hedgehog.

So, Dog went to fetch what he needed, his provisions.

'Right, let's see … a bathing suit, a bucket and spade, dark glasses and fur screen, a good book, my sailor's hat, my fishing rod. Oh, and my favourite rug.' The Dog then scurried back to his garden and looked at what he had collected. 'Oh dear,' he said 'I'm so mixed up today I need my satchel, for goodness sake,

Silly Dog. How else would I transport my special things?'

He stopped and thought. 'This is so exhausting. I think I'll have some dinner. It's just about that time and my tummy's rumbling.

I'm quite peckish after all that searching for very important things.'
So, Dog went inside his house to fetch his dinner.

'Ah, a lovely fresh salad and bones, perfect for a day like today.
I think I'll eat it in the garden since it's such a warm evening,' he
said licking his lips with delight. So Dog sat down to his dinner and
enjoyed every last bit of it. When he had finished, he lay back in
his chair and imagined all the possibilities for his day away. The
beach, the seaside, the forest, the babbling brook, his Aunt's
cottage ... 'I know', said the dog 'As I picture my adventure, I shall
picture each place and what I see most clearly will be where I shall
go. Let me see, seashells, the sand, the berries, the woods.'

As the dog lay back in his chair, he had barely imagined the golden
sands of the beach when he began to dream and fell fast asleep.

Two minutes later a neighbouring Beagle and a good friend of Dog
passed by. He knocked at the front door. No reply. He rang the
bell. No reply. He shouted through letterbox.

'Hello ... anybody there, Dog?'

No reply.

Beagle noticed that the garden gate was open and he pushed it
gently and went round to the back of the house. 'Ah, there you are,

old friend. I wondered if you were free for a chat.' On saying that, Beagle patted Dog on his head.

'Ah! Oh ha-ha. What a fright you gave me, I didn't hear you come in,' said Dog with happiness.

'I didn't mean to startle you. I did knock but there was no reply,' said Beagle apologetically. 'I just wondered if you fancied a chat.'

'Of course,' replied Dog. 'What a wonderful surprise! But I haven't got long as I plan to go away for the day.'

'Really,' said Beagle, 'for the day you say. Don't you think it's rather late, my friend?'

'Late? Why what time is it now?' asked Dog.

'It's nearly bedtime, dear Dog.'

'Oh , how very disappointing. Are you sure Beagle? I so wanted to go away for the day,' whimpered Dog, who was very disappointed.

Beagle put his paws around Dog's shoulders and said, 'Oh well, not to worry. I was also planning to go away today but you know, I just couldn't make up my mind which was the best place to visit.'

'I just couldn't make up my mind either. I ended up lying out in my garden all day.' With this comment Dog started to laugh. 'What a couple of silly-billies we are sweet Beagle. I shall go and make us a couple of cool drinks.' 'Perfect, thank you,' said Beagle. And with that Dog bustled inside He was looking forward to hearing about his chum's imaginary adventures.

The two friends sat in the cool night air and discussed the difficulties of making up one's mind and decision making in general. 'Yes,' said dog 'but do you know, I'm glad that I didn't go away after all.'

'Why ever not?' asked Beagle

'Because,' said Dog shyly, 'if I had, I wouldn't have seen you and we wouldn't have spent this time together and enjoyed our chat on this beautiful evening in my garden.'

'Oh, what a lovely thing to say,' said Beagle blushing.

'It's true Beagle, for I could have gone to many places today but now I realise that I was just as happy staying at home and finishing off a perfect day talking with my best friend.'

'Thank you,' said Beagle I agree completely.

Funny thing is, I was coming round to ask your advice on what you thought was the best place to go on such a bright and sunny day.'

'And now we know,' said the Dog 'Home sweet home.'

The two friends sat for hours until the sun started to rise again. 'I wonder if today will be fine' said Beagle. 'We should go away for the day,' laughed Dog.

BRAIN TEASER /WHAT DO YOU REMEMBER?

How many animals are in this story?

_____

What symbol was on Dogs collar?

_____

Was the weather sunny or rainy?

_____

Who was Dogs best friend?

_____

How many places did Dog dream of?

_____

_____

_____

Give three items that Dog put in his satchel (bag)

_____

_____

_____

What have you learned about the animals?

A They are nasty to each other.

_____

Or

B They care for each other?

_____

Acknowledgements

My Mum, Helen Letters

My sisters Carole and Suzy Letters

Sean Houghton

Fran Rodriguez

Alan Park

Thank you for all your support and belief

Also to:

Ian R. Ward for his fabulous illustrations

Written by I-J Letters

(On One of Those Days)
© 2020
Illustrated by Ian R Ward

Lightning Source UK Ltd.
Milton Keynes UK
UKHW050253011220
374383UK00005B/276